PUFFIN BOOKS

Admiral Fatso Fitzpugwash

John Ryan was born in Edinburgh and spent much
of his early life abroad and at boarding school in
England. After war service in Burma he taught
art at Harrow and became a contributor to *Eagle*
magazine, then in its infancy. Captain Pugwash,
who later became his most famous creation on
television and in picture books, was in fact created
for *Eagle*. Other characters include Harris Tweed,
Lettice Leefe, Mary, Mungo and Midge, Sir
Prancelot and Fatso the Fathead.

John Ryan is married with three children and
several grandchildren. He lives in Rye, Sussex, a
one-time notorious haunt of smugglers and
pirates. He hopes to continue writing and drawing
indefinitely . . . if only to avoid being put to work
in the garden!

D1363160

Admiral Fatso FitzPugwash

John Ryan

Admiral Fatso FitzPugwash

PUFFIN BOOKS

PUFFIN BOOKS

Published by the Penguin Group
Penguin Books Ltd, 27 Wrights Lane, London W8 5TZ, England
Penguin Books USA Inc., 375 Hudson Street, New York, New York 10014, USA
Penguin Books Australia Ltd, Ringwood, Victoria, Australia
Penguin Books Canada Ltd, 10 Alcorn Avenue, Toronto, Ontario, Canada M4V 3B2
Penguin Books (NZ) Ltd, 182–190 Wairau Road, Auckland 10, New Zealand

Penguin Books Ltd, Registered Offices: Harmondsworth, Middlesex, England

First published by Viking 1994
Published in Puffin Books 1995
3 5 7 9 10 8 6 4

Printed in England by Clays Ltd, St. Ives plc

Contents

Admiral
Fatso

Chapter One

The King of England was in a bad temper. His enemies, the French, had once again invaded the English coast and looted everything in sight.

"We need some defences!" he shouted. "Haven't we got a Baron or somebody . . .

. . . somebody who can *do* something about it?"

The Queen looked doubtful. "Well, there *is* Fatso," she said, "I mean, the Baron Fatsophilus FitzPugwash. It's about time he did something useful."

"Fatso! Fatso
the Fathead!"
roared the King.
"He's useless!
Greedy, stupid,
cowardly . . . !"

"But he's *there*,
dear," replied the
Queen. "He's
about the only
Baron we've got
in those parts."

"Oh, very well," said the King crossly. "I suppose he's better than nobody. I'll make him an Admiral. I'll send him a really big medal to prove it. He's so greedy he'll do anything for a bit of gold and silver!"

In his cosy castle in the little port of Winkle, the Baron Fatsophilus FitzPugwash, Fatso to his friends and Fatso the Fathead to everybody else, was enjoying his afternoon tea, when his servant, Fiddle, brought in the royal parcel.

"When is a packet not a packet, Sir?" asked Fiddle, who loved jokes and riddles.

"Dunno!" said the Baron.

"When you *un*-pack it," said Fiddle. "Wah hah hah!"

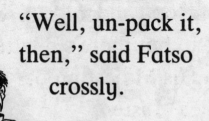

"Well, un-pack it, then," said Fatso crossly.

But when he saw what was
inside, the Baron's eyes
glittered greedily.

"A medal . . . gold – silver
. . . for *me* . . . from the
King!" he breathed happily.

"About time I was rewarded
for my long and faithful service."

"Ah, but there's a letter
from His Majesty too," said
Fiddle. "Listen."

And Fiddle read:

"To the Baron Fatsophilus
FitzPugwash. Greetings. His
Royal Majesty the King
hereby appoints you Lord
High Admiral of his Fleet
and sends you this medal in
token of your office.
Furthermore the King and
Queen will visit and inspect
you on board your flagship
one month hence."

When he heard this, Fatso
turned pale. Being an Admiral
sounded dangerous. And the
Baron couldn't *stand* water.

As a baby
he had kicked and
scratched when
anybody tried
to bath him.

As a child he
had refused to
paddle with the
other children.

"I can't do it," he said. "I can't stand water – and we haven't *even* got a ship!"

"Yes, but you can't disobey the King, either," said Fiddle. "But not to worry . . . we'll *build* you a ship. Just like the one on the medal."

"Hm," said Fatso. "But supposing it sinks? With *me* on board!"

"I've got an idea about that too," said Fiddle.

"Bagseye the Beggar!

Haven't you ever noticed? Clean him up a bit and he looks exactly like YOU! We'll dress him up, and on the day he can take your place."

"Fiddle, you're a wonder!"
shouted Fatso. "Lead me to
him!"

Bagseye the Beggar was
outside, sitting on the castle
steps. He looked very dirty and
ill-tempered. You could see the
fleas jumping all over him.

But he cheered up when
Fiddle explained his plan.

"Yer, well, sounds all right,"
said Bagseye . . .

"Only I'll 'ave to move into
the castle straight away, an'
live an' dress like the Baron, to
get used to playin' 'is part,
like."

"Then there'll be my fee. Let's say fifty gold crowns, up front."

The Baron was very mean. He *hated* paying anybody . . .

. . . but anything was better than getting his feet wet . . .

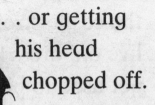

. . . or getting his head chopped off.

So he paid out the fifty crowns, and Bagseye the Beggar moved into the castle.

That day, Fiddle and his friends started work on the Admiral's flagship

and Fatso set to work on
Bagseye. It wasn't easy.

Extra staff had to be hired to wash him and shave him.

(The fleas were sold to a performing flea company.)

His smart new clothes cost a
fortune . . .

. . . and he ate and he ate,
and he drank and he drank,
until he began to look very like
Fatso indeed.

In fact, by the day before the King's arrival . . .

. . . you could hardly tell the difference.

Chapter Two

Next morning, the new flagship was ready. It did look *exactly* like the one on the King's medal.

A crowd had gathered on the quayside to wait for the Royal arrival.

Then a cry went up from the battlements:

"The King's party is in sight. Stand by to receive Their Majesties!"

Inside the castle, Fatso was
giving Bagseye his final orders.
"Is everything absolutely
clear?" he asked anxiously.

"Yer, but I'll 'ave to wear
the medal," said Bagseye.

"Hm, yes, well, er, um, I
suppose so. But mind you
guard it well," said the Baron.
"Now, get down there quick.
Don't keep Their Majesties
waiting."

And the Baron took up his position at one of the castle windows to watch. The King's party arrived at the quayside.

The ship gleamed, the water
sparkled . . . the crowd waited
eagerly.

Only the King looked
impatient. What had happened
to his new Lord High Admiral?

Fatso was wondering
too. Where on earth was
Bagseye?

Then Fiddle rushed in.

"It's Bagseye, Mr Baron,
Sir," he cried.

"HE'S GONE!!"

"Ah, there you are at last,
Fatso," said the King. "What a
splendid new flagship you
have. Come, let us go aboard."

38

There was nothing Fatso
could do. He climbed the steps,
shut his eyes, held his nose . . .

and stepped
on board.

But then a strange thing happened. The end of the ship he was standing on suddenly sank down under his weight

. . . leaving him floating.
Poor Fatso thought his last
hour really *had* come.

But then the *other* end of the
ship came up and over, and
landed on top of him.

Luckily, there was a
hatchway which exactly fitted
him. When the ship righted
itself . . .

. . . there was
Fatso stuck in
the hatchway
like a cork in a barrel. All you
could see was his bottom half,
kicking.

The King and Queen roared
with laughter.

So did the
crowd.

"'Pon my oath, Fatso," cried the Monarch. "That was the funniest sight I've ever seen! Maybe you ought to be my Court Jester!

"That reminds me, the French have promised never to invade us again. I won't need a fleet after all . . . *or* an Admiral.

"So *you* won't need that medal I sent you. Can I have it back?"

"The medal, Your Majesty?" stammered Fatso.

"Well, er, um, er, *actually* I gave it to a poor beggar-man. His need was, er, greater than mine."

"A fine and generous act, Fatso," said the King as they left. "Perhaps you're not such a bad fellow after all!"

The Baron breathed a sigh of relief. He hadn't drowned and he wasn't an Admiral.

"I got away with it after all!"

"Ah," said Fiddle, "but the one who really *did* get away with it . . .

" . . . was Bagseye the Beggar!"

Fatso and the Feast

Chapter One

It had been a bad winter in Winkle, cold and dark, wet and windy. All the townsfolk were miserable.

Nobody had any money.

The bread was stale, the vegetables were rotten and the milk was sour.

There wasn't even anything to drink at the inn.

The Travelling Players couldn't put on their show . . .

because nobody had any money to pay for the tickets.

Even when spring came
people didn't cheer up.

The only person who was
comfortable and contented . . .

. . . was the Baron Fatso FitzPugwash. *He* had everything: plenty of cream cakes and wine . . .

. . . a fine warm fire, and his servant, Fiddle, to look after him. He was also *very* rich.

Far below, in the dungeons,
the Baron kept
masses of gold
and silver. He
spent a lot of
his time
counting it.

He was far too mean to give any
of it away. He thought nothing
of the poor townspeople . . .

. . . and they
thought nothing
of him.

"Isn't there anything you
can do about that master of
yours, Fiddle?" asked Alfred
the Actor. "He's so *stingy*!"

"String 'im up,
I says," shouted
Butch the Baddy
from his prison
cell.

"No, no, that would
never do!" cried
Fiddle. "I'd lose
my job!"

"I know
something that
might work," said Annie the
Actor's daughter . . .

Listen...

A few days later, a fearful storm broke over the town.

The people shivered in their houses, but Fatso sat warm and snug in the castle parlour.

Suddenly, he heard a loud knocking. The window flew open. There on the sill was a hideous old woman, clutching a broomstick and a big black cat.

"Wh-who are you?" stammered the Baron.

"A witch, of course," cackled the old crone. "Forced down on my broomstick, by the storm. Terrible weather you have in these parts.

"I'm looking for a night's shelter. How about asking me in?"

"C-certainly not, you horrible old hag," cried Fatso. He was *terrified* of witches.

But she said, "You'd better, or I'll turn you into a toad. Watch that cat!"

62

There was a bright flash, a
cloud of smoke . . .

. . . and when it cleared the
cat had gone. In its place sat
an ugly toad.

"See what I mean?" said the
witch. Fatso did see. He was
terrified of toads too, especially
talking toads!

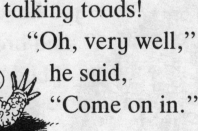

Evenin' Baron

"Oh, very well,"
he said,
"Come on in."

"And now for a nice hot
supper," said the old woman.
"I'm hungry!" It was Fiddle's
day off, so
Fatso had to
cook and
serve the
whole meal
himself.

"Not bad," said the witch.
"Now, the best bedroom
you have, please,
and breakfast in
bed tomorrow."

But next morning, when
Fatso came with the breakfast,
the bed was empty, the window
open and the witch gone.

"Heaven be praised," said Fatso to Fiddle. "She threatened to turn me into a . . . "

"Into a TOAD," laughed Fiddle. "And *you* TOED the line! Wah hah hah!"

But Fatso didn't think it was at all funny.

And next morning, when he woke up, the witch was back, toad and all.

"I've got some news for you," she said.

"Message from the King himself!"

"Oh, no!" cried Fatso. "What would *you* be doing with the King's messages?"

"She's a friend of 'is," croaked the toad.

"The King's Messengers are all on strike," said the witch,

"so I've come instead.

S'right!

"The King says he intends to pay a State Visit to you, here in Winkle, on May Day. There's to be a great feast, music, merry-making and play-acting and lots of food and drink for him and all his court."

"All his *court*," said Fatso, turning white. "How many is that?"

"Oh, about a thousand . . . keeps a big court, does our King," cackled the witch.

"B-but who's going to *pay*?" stammered the Baron.

"Why – *you*, of course," said the witch, "unless you want to lose your head. Now I must fly. Ta ta!"

And with another flash and a cloud of smoke, she was gone.

Poor Baron Fatso. The King and a *thousand* guests! It would cost a fortune and *he* would have to pay for the lot!

But the King's orders had to be obeyed.

Everybody seemed
surprisingly ready and
willing to help.

The Bakers baked . . .

The bread and cakes and
pies were the tastiest ever
known in the town.

The Farmers brought in the best spring vegetables,

and the Fishermen fished day and night.

The Musicians practised their music.

The Players rehearsed their acts.

A splendid maypole was set up . . .

and Fatso paid . . .

The day before May Day, everything was ready and the Baron was feeling very poor indeed.

Welcome to Winkle

"Looks good, doesn't it?" said Fiddle. "Very nice for the King and his court, that's what I say."

But at that moment, Fatso
felt a hand on his arm.

"It's me, dearie," said the
witch. "Flown in from London
again. I've got another
message from His Majesty."

"He says his fortune-teller (that's me) has told him tomorrow's not such a good day to visit Winkle after all. So he's not coming!

"BUT, knowing all the trouble you've taken, he says he wants all the townspeople to have the party instead and enjoy all the goodies you've prepared for him."

"Hurrah, hurrah!" shouted all the townsfolk. "Three cheers for His Majesty!"

"All my lovely money wasted," thought Fatso miserably, but there was nothing for it because . . .

when he turned to look for the witch, she was gone.

Next morning, the party
began. Everybody ate and
drank far more than was good
for them.

Even Fatso decided to make
the best of it and joined in.

Everybody danced round
and round the maypole.

Even
Fatso.

The Actors put
on their show,
and Fatso loved
it.

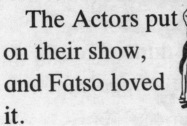

The Musicians played their music

and he
liked that too.
Everybody had
a wonderful
time.

"Three cheers for the Baron," cried Fiddle. And the people of Winkle picked up Fatso and carried him shoulder-high through the town.

It was as they passed the back of the Actor's tent that he noticed . . .

a mask just like the witch's face, a broomstick, a cat and a toad.

Alfredo the Actor, Annie his daughter, the Conjuror and the Ventriloquist were sitting having a good laugh with Fiddle.

"Wh-where . . .
wh-what . . . what
is all this?"
spluttered the
Baron.

"Oh dear, he's spotted us,
Fiddle," said Alfredo.
"Perhaps we'd better tell him
the truth.

"You see," he said to Fatso,
"we all wanted a party . . .

"Annie here, is a very good actress. On the night of the storm she put on this mask and dressed up as the witch.

"Then up the ladder she went, to your window. Ventro and Congo followed behind, only *you* couldn't see them.

"Annie did the talking, and Congo made the flash and the smoke . . .

while they
swapped the
toad for the cat.

"Then Ventro did the toad's voice . . . and you believed all of it!"

"I know it was a dirty trick to play on you, Sir, but we *have* all had a lovely party!"

Fatso knew he ought to be furious, but he wasn't. Maybe the money had not been wasted after all.

"Dirty trick?" he cried. "Nonsense! I've enjoyed every minute of it!

Well done, everybody!" And he danced round the maypole all night long.

Also in Young Puffin

PUGWASH
AND THE MIDNIGHT FEAST
PUGWASH
AND THE WRECKERS

John Ryan

"Havin' a midnight feast, eh?" roared
Jake, "and never thought of askin' *us*
to join you?"

Captain Pugwash and his crew are
interrupted eating their midnight feast by
some very unwelcome visitors – Cut-
throat Jake and his bloodthirsty
buccaneers! The greedy villains take
over, but not for long...And there's more
crafty plotting from the evil Jake when
he sets out to wreck the *Black Pig*, full of
the biggest load of bullion ever!